Talking
to
Faith
Ringgold

by

Faith Ringgold,

Linda Freeman

& Nancy Roucher

Crown Publishers, Inc.
New York

Copyright © 1996 by Faith Ringgold,
Linda Freeman & Nancy Roucher

All rights reserved. No part of this book may be
reproduced or transmitted in any form or by any
means, electronic or mechanical, including
photocopying, recording, or by any information
storage and retrieval system, without permission in
writing from the publisher.

Published by Crown Publishers, Inc.,
a Random House company, 201 East 50th Street,
New York, New York 10022

CROWN is a trademark of Crown Publishers, Inc.

Manufactured in the United States of America

Library of Congress Cataloging-in-Publication Data

Ringgold, Faith.
Talking to Faith Ringgold / by Faith Ringgold,
Linda Freeman & Nancy Roucher. — 1st ed.
p. cm.
Includes index.
Summary: An interactive biography of the African-
American artist and children's book author, detailing
her experiences, perspectives, and the inspiration for
her art. At intervals in the text, the reader is asked
related questions.
1. Ringgold, Faith—Juvenile literature. 2. Afro-
American artists—Biography—Juvenile literature.
[1. Ringgold, Faith. 2. Artists. 3. Afro-Americans—
Biography. 4. Women—Biography. 5. Art
appreciation.] I. Freeman, Linda. II. Roucher, Nancy.
III. Title.
N6537.R55A2   1995a
                                    709'.2—dc20
[B]
                            95-23455

ISBN 0-517-88546-8 (pbk.)
0-517-70914-7 (lib. bdg.)

10 9 8 7 6 5 4 3 2 1

First Edition

Picture credits: Page 3: by Linda Freeman,
courtesy of Faith Ringgold. 4: Faith Ringgold.
5: UPI/Bettmann. 6, 7, 9: Faith Ringgold *except* 9,
bottom right: Michael James. 11: The Textile Museum,
Washington, D.C., courtesy of Faith Ringgold. 12: Faith
Ringgold. 13: Courtesy, Museum of Fine Arts, Boston.
14, 15, 16: Faith Ringgold. 17: The Textile Museum,
Washington, D.C., courtesy of Faith Ringgold.
18: Faith Ringgold. 20, top right: UPI/Bettmann.
21: The Bettmann Archive. 22: Faith Ringgold.
24, 25: UPI/Bettmann *except* 24, bottom right:
Declan Haun/Black Star. 26, 27, 28: Faith Ringgold.
31: The Bettmann Archive. 32: Faith Ringgold.
34, top left: The Bettmann Archive. 34, top right:
AP/Wide World Photos. 34, bottom left: courtesy of
the Schomburg Collection. 34, bottom right:
UPI/Bettmann. 35, top left: courtesy of the
Schomburg Collection. 35, top right: The Bettmann
Archive. 35, bottom left: UPI/Bettmann. 35, bottom
right: AP/Wide World. 36, right, 37: Scala/Art
Resource, New York. 39: The Bettmann Archive.
40, 41, 45: Faith Ringgold.

I am inspired by people who rise above their adversity. That's my deepest inspiration. And also I'm inspired by the fact that if I really, really want to, I think I can do anything.

Introduce yourself...

Who are you? Write a brief biography. Include the facts (name, age, where you were born, where you live). But most important, describe yourself. What makes you "you"? What do you like to do?

Who influenced you?

Is there a special person in your life who influenced you—the way Faith Ringgold's mother influenced her? Describe an incident that illustrates this.

With mother in Harlem, about 1933.

Harlem, 135th Street and
Lenox Avenue, about 1930.

Introducing Myself

I have always lived in Harlem

or very close to it. I was born in central Harlem in 1930. We lived on 146th Street. When I was 12 years old, we moved up to 150th Street and Edgecombe Avenue on Sugar Hill. Until recently, I lived on 145th Street and Edgecombe. I still have a studio there, but my home is now just a few minutes from Harlem, over the George Washington Bridge in Englewood, New Jersey.

I grew up during the time of the Great Depression, when many people didn't have jobs or money. Because I had asthma, I never went to kindergarten. I don't remember going to first grade. I really started going to school in the second grade. And even then I was out a lot with asthma. So I was *very* carefully brought up. And my mother taught me a lot, took me to museums. She also took me to fun places like the Paramount. I saw all the stars—Duke Ellington, Billie Holiday, Ella Fitzgerald. So I think, in a way of speaking, that art to me in the beginning was not painting. It was performing. I got a chance to see how someone can communicate to large groups of people. And I think I wanted to reach people too.

Now, as I said, I was sick. I would be in bed recuperating from asthma, and my mother would give me not only my schoolbooks but I would get paper and crayons to draw and I would get bits of cloth and needle and thread and I would make little things. My mother was a fashion designer and a dressmaker and so cloth and sewing were always there.

5

Tar Beach, 1988

Tar Beach

If you look closely at *Tar Beach,* you may learn more about me.

It's really about going up to the roof, which has a tar floor, in the summertime

when I was a child. My father would take the mattress up and my mother would

place a sheet on it and some pillows and we kids would lie on the mattress.

It was very hot and we could have food up there—watermelon and fried chicken and all kinds

of goodies. The adults would play cards and the children would lie there and listen to them

talking. And it was cool. I wrote about this little girl in the picture who is dreaming that she owns

all the skyscraper buildings that she can see from the roof and the George Washington Bridge.

She imagines that she can fly and that she can make life better for her family.

With my older sister, Barbara, on Tar Beach, 1936.

Faith Ringgold's painting of *Tar Beach* was based on a memory from her childhood.
Part of it really happened and part of it—about the little girl flying—is a fantasy that she made up.
Do you have a memory of something that happened to you when you were younger?
Draw or describe what happened. Add a fantasy or dream to change the story.

7

Growing Up

Looking back at the 1930s,

people didn't ask little girls what they wanted to be when they grew up. It was kind of assumed that you were going to be a wife and mommy, you know?

Now, my mother wanted us to be somebody out there in the world. So what we knew and what we were trained to think about was that we were going to college. That was definite. But it wasn't said what we were going to be. My family had no idea I would be an artist.

I had a professor at the City College of New York, where I graduated with a degree in art, who never once told me that he didn't like my drawings. At the end of the semester, we had a series of four drawings to do as a test. One of them had to do with mountains. Now, I was born and raised in New York City and in the summers we went to the seashore, so the mountains I don't know about, okay? So I did these mountains and I gave them to him and he said, "What are *these*?" And I said, "Those are mountains." So he said, "Write it on there." I said, "Does this mean you don't think I can draw? I plan to be an artist." He said, "Well, I don't see any indications that you can."

So when he said, "You can't be an artist, you can't draw," I said, "Oh, yes, I can. I *definitely* can." I mean, I wasn't sure whether I could, but now I can—just 'cause you say I can't.

Did anyone ever tell you that you didn't have the ability to do something you really wanted to do? Describe the incident. How did it make you feel?
Can you think of how you can still do what you want? What would help you? What would stop you?

Faith,
Barbara,
Andrew,
1931.

Barbara,
Andrew, Faith,
1938.

Faith (center)
and friends,
Atlantic City,
1945.

High school graduation, 1948.

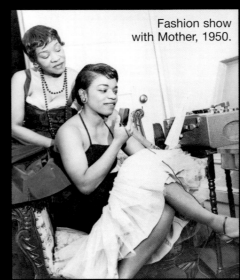

Fashion show
with Mother, 1950.

Faith, Burdette Ringgold (left),
and best man, 1960.

Lecturing,
1974.

With
granddaughter
Faith, 1989.

6

Paris studio, 1990.

About Being an Artist

At college I was taught to copy Greek busts and I was taught to copy Cézanne and Rembrandt and so on, because that was the way they did it then. Later I had to unlearn that. Not *un*learn it, because I still know it—but

I had to find out what *my* art was going to look like.

In trying to develop my own art, I would mix my European training with my knowledge of classical African art and that would be my African-American art—and that is me, because I am a composite of my African roots and my American-European culture. So I went to museums, I bought books on African art, and I copied again. I copied!

In this copying, I deliberately made the heads of people more prominent—in African art the head is considered the seat of wisdom—and used bold, flat shapes. I learned a lot about African design—symmetry, repetition, pattern, texture, and so on—and then I incorporated these elements in my art, which became not African art but African-American art. And I used it to express not the African experience, which I didn't have, but the African-American experience—and that's what my art *really* is. It's an expression of the African-American-female experience.

A Faith Ringgold soft sculpture and an African fabric.

A Faith Ringgold soft sculpture and an African mask.

What can you learn by copying?
Find out for yourself by copying a famous bust or painting.

Do you think it's okay to copy? For what reasons?

—Exhibited at the **Textile Museum in Washington, D.C., 1993.**

Quilt-making

Susie Shannon, about 1900.

This quilt was made in the 1880s
by an African-American woman
named Harriet Powers,
who was born into slavery in 1837.

The African-American woman is credited with the beginning of quilt-making in America. She did it as part of her duties as a slave girl, making covers for the family.

Quilts are part of my own family tradition.

My mother remembered watching her grandmother Betsy Bingham boil and bleach flour sacks until they were "white as snow" to line the quilts she made. My great-great-grandmother Susie Shannon (Betsy's mother) had taught her to sew quilts. She was a slave and made quilts for the plantation owners as part of her duties as a house girl.

In African art, utilitarian objects were made beautiful. So the slave women incorporated traditional African designs on these coverlets and created in America what we today call the quilt. This would mean that quilt-making is like jazz: both were begun by African-Americans. In the case of jazz, by African-American men, and in the case of quilts, by African-American women. They constitute two original contributions made by Americans to the world.

Make it beautiful . . .
Draw an everyday, utilitarian object and embellish it with African designs.

13

Is It Art ?

What do you think "real" art is?

My soft sculptures began as dolls, then masks, then hanging figures, and then free-standing sculptures. *Mrs. Jones and Family*, from the "Family of Woman" mask series, is a "portrait" of my family. I did it in 1973. My mother made the clothes.

In the late 1960s, when I began thinking about incorporating various forms of African art into my own—like fabric and beading—people wanted to know, what is this?

Is this real art, or is this some sort of folk tradition that you're using here?

Martin Luther King, 1975

I think art is serious if it is based on something you know about and have experienced—if there are important ideas involved, as opposed to just imitating the art of others for lack of an idea of your own, like weaving a basket from a kit. Whether it is traditional or modern or cutting-edge or whatever isn't important. Does it communicate to people? *That's* what's important in art.

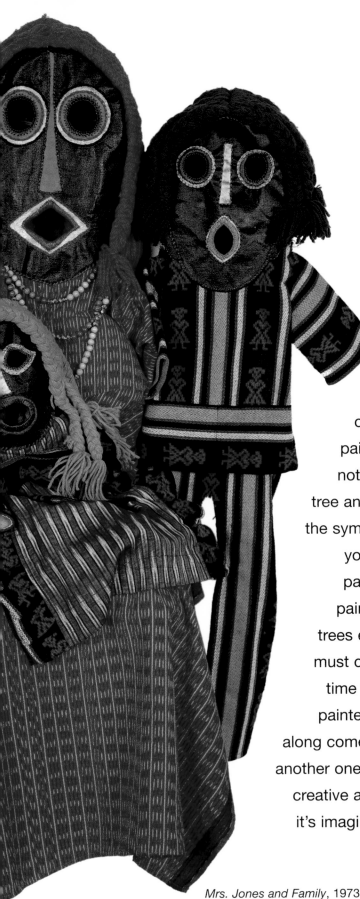

Art Is Hard Work

Making art has to hold your interest because as an artist you need to repeat the process over and over again. If you're painting a tree, you're not going to paint one tree and have that one be the symbol for all the trees you are ever going to paint. You're going to paint different kinds of trees everywhere, so you must continue. And every time you think you have painted the ultimate tree, along comes another one and another one and another. Art is creative and it's exciting and it's imaginative. But it's hard work.

How many different ways can you draw a tree, a bird, or any other object?
From the back, side, above, below?
Will you use thick lines or thin lines? Dark or light colors? Shading or outlining? Patterns and textures or flat colors?
Think of all the possibilities and then draw your object several ways.

Mrs. Jones and Family, 1973

Solving a Problem

When I was starting out, there were hardly any galleries that showed the work of black women or women in general.

I had slides,

and in case the gallery

didn't have time to look at slides,

I had photographs with me,

and in case

they couldn't look at the photographs,

I had the work itself!

I had an opportunity to show my work provided I could ship it easily. Framed paintings have to be packed in crates, which are heavy and expensive to ship. In Amsterdam, Holland, I saw several examples of Tibetan *tankas*, which are paintings that are framed in cloth. I thought this was an excellent alternative to framing paintings in wood, because the painting could be rolled up and placed in a trunk and shipped rather inexpensively. So when I got home I shared the idea with my mother and she started making cloth frames.

And it worked. I got a lot of exhibitions and lectures for which I was paid. Then I decided to write stories and put them on my paintings. So I became a full-time artist and I also got an audience all over the country.

With Mother,
working on my first painted quilt,
Echoes of Harlem,
in 1980.

A Faith Ringgold
cloth-framed painting (left)
and a Tibetan *tanka.*

—Exhibited at the
Textile Museum in Washington, D.C.,
1993.

Sonny's Quilt, 1986

Seeing, Thinking, Planning Like an Artist

Look at *Sonny's Quilt.*
Analyze the composition.
Name everything you see.
Let your eye roam around the picture.
How is it composed? What is the most important thing in the painting? What draws your eye to it? Think about relationships—size, color, line, shape, perspective, and space.

Composition in a work of art is very important and very difficult. It's always a problem—where to put what in the picture, what to show, how to show it, what angle to show it at, and then what colors to make everything. So there's the color composition and the spatial composition. There's the content—there are all these different things that go on in a picture.

19

Sonny Rollins, 1962.

**What do you think
Sonny's Quilt is about?**
What kind of mood or feeling
does this picture convey?

**Draw a scene with a
surprise.**
In *Sonny's Quilt,* everything is
anchored in the city. What
you don't expect to see is a
man playing a saxophone on
the bridge. Can you create a
similarly surprising scene?

20

**I think quilt-makers,
who are famous
for taking
little squares of cloth
and
sewing them together,
have created
a brilliant way
to deal with space.**

That's essential to what I'm trying to do here—reducing space to small squares that are put together into a larger space and then quilted with lines of stitching that bisect each square into two or more triangles. Then bordering those squares are smaller squares that are composed of triangles, which are pieced together to form one or more borders around the entire quilt. It's just such a simple but ingenious idea that comes to us from quilting and I use it in my painting.

The bridge actually makes me think of quilts. Do you know why? Because it has the same kind of construction of squares and triangles. A quilt is put together with squares and triangles, and so are the towers of the bridge.

This piece is about the famous jazz musician Sonny Rollins, who also grew up in Harlem. He had this habit of practicing in strange places—on rooftops, fire escapes, and in this case a bridge!

The
Brooklyn
Bridge

Ideas

Art is about more than just technique or style. It's about ideas.

How do I get my ideas? You can look at my work and see what has inspired me and how it has changed over time.

This is *The Flag Is Bleeding,* painted in 1967. What was happening when I painted this? I was responding to events around me. . . .

The Flag Is Bleeding, 1967

In the **1960s**, civil rights protests began in many American cities.▲ ▶

In **1963**, John F. Kennedy and Medgar Evers ▲ were assassinated, and four black girls were killed when a bomb exploded in a church in Birmingham, Alabama.▼ Two hundred thousand people attended a march on Washington and heard Martin Luther King, Jr., tell of his dream for freedom for all people! ▶

In **1962,** James Meredith became the first African-American student at the University of Mississippi.▼

In **1964**, three young civil rights workers were murdered. Dr. King received the Nobel Peace Prize for his nonviolent leadership.

Analyze
The Flag Is Bleeding.
What do you see that tells you about racial conflict and discrimination? How is the painting composed? What is most important? Why is the flag in this painting? What is its message?

In **1965**, many African-Americans staged riots in cities to show their anger over discrimination and the lack of jobs. ▲ The Vietnam War escalated.

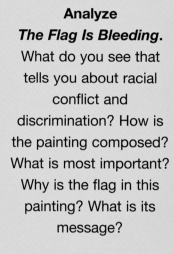

In **1966**, the Black Power movement began, calling for black pride, rediscovering the African heritage, and meeting violence with retaliation.▼

What is happening in the world today that you feel strongly about?
Create your own artwork that shows how you feel.

25

Dancing at the Louvre

I combine real people from my life and things I have done with influences from art history. On my first trip to Europe, I went with my mother and two young daughters. Thirty years later, I had an opportunity to go to France and stay there for a while. And I decided to do some painting that focuses on the African-American experience in France.

This series is called the French Collection and it's like my first novel.

The paintings are about a young woman named Willia Marie Simone. She goes to Paris in 1920 when she's sixteen. She becomes an artist, an artist's model, and the owner of a café, where she hosts the famous French artists.

Willia Marie is my alter ego. She is also somewhat like my mother, as my mother was a fabulous woman who would definitely have gone to Paris

Setting sail for France on the S.S. Liberté.

in the twenties if she could have, and probably would have been a dancer, because that's what she wanted to do. Willia's story is a fantasy—about things we've never done but would like to have done.

Wedding on the Seine

Matisse's Chapel

Dinner at Gertrude Stein's

On the Beach at St. Tropez

Café des Artistes

Some chapters from the French Collection, 1991.

In *Dancing at the Louvre,* I tell a story about a friend of Willia Marie's named Marcia, who takes her—along with her own three children—to the Louvre in Paris, which is probably the most famous art museum in the world.

(By the way, the children in the picture are really my grandchildren and Marcia is my daughter, but not in the story.)

*Dancing
at the Louvre,*
1991

**What is the mood of
Dancing at the Louvre?**
Is it joyous, serious,
funny, realistic, fantastic?
Why?

It's kind of a joke, you know.

I mean, nobody but a very gauche

American would dance at the

Louvre. If you want to find out what

the joke is, you have to know

something about art history.

Do you see anything in this artwork that you recognize?

The *Mona Lisa* is one of the most admired works of art in history.

Leonardo da Vinci (1452-1519) was not only an artist but also an inventor. He recorded his ideas in pages of sketches in his notebooks. One of his greatest achievements was the *Mona Lisa,* where he expertly used the new medium of oil paint and the techniques of perspective, use of light and shadow, and symmetrical composition. Can you see how he has used a triangle to focus your eye directly on the Mona Lisa? Trace from the Mona Lisa's head down one arm, across, and then up the other arm.

But it's the Mona Lisa's smile that is so mysterious and has fascinated people over so many centuries.

What do you think the Mona Lisa would say if she could see Marcia and her children dancing at the Louvre?

Leonardo da Vinci, *Mona Lisa,* 1503-5

THE SUNFLOWERS QUILTING BEE AT ARLES

The National Sunflower Quilters Society of America are having quilting bees in sunflower fields around the world to spread the cause of freedom. Aunt Melissa has written to inform me of this and to say; "Go with them to the sunflower fields in Arles. And please take care of them in that foreign country, Willa Marie. These women are our freedom," she write.

1. Today the women arrived in Arles. They are Madame Walker, Sojourner Truth, Ida Wells, Fannie Lou Hamer, Harriet Tubman, Rosa Parks, Mary McLeod Bethune and Ella Baker, a fortress of African American women's courage, with enough energy to transform a nation piece by piece.

2. Look what they've done in spite of their oppression: Madame Walker invented the hair straightening comb and became the first self-made American-born woman billionaire. She employed over 3,000 people. Sojourner Truth spoke up brilliantly for women's rights during slavery, and could neither read nor write. Ida Wells made an expose of the horror of lynching in the South.

3. Fannie Lou Hamer braved police dogs, water hoses, brutal beatings, and jail in order to register thousands of people to vote. Harriet Tubman braved over 300 slaves to freedom in 19 trips from the South on the Underground Railroad during slavery and never lost a passenger. Rosa Parks became the mother of the Civil Rights movement when she sat down in the front of a segregated bus and refused to move to the back.

4. Mary McLeod Beth[...] special advisor [...] Roosevelt Ella Bak[...] the condition of p[...] trip to Arles was [...] symbol of their [...]

7. "He's the image of the man that hit me in the head with a rock when I was a girl," Harriet said. "Made him scary. He reminds me of slavery." But he was not about to be moved. Like one of the sunflowers, he appeared to be growing out of the ground. Sojourner slipt into the stitches of her quilting, for the loss of her fourteen children mostly all sold into slavery.

8. One of Sojourner's children, a girl, was sold to a Dutch slaver in the West Indies who then took her to Holland. "Was that something this Dutch man might know sometimes about?" she conceited about you, Willa Marie. "Is this a natural setting for a black woman?" Sojourner asked.

9. "I came to France to seek opportunity," I said. "It is not possible for me to be an artist in the states," "We are all artists. Piecing is our art. We bring art to everyday life in Africa," they said. "That was what we did after a hard day's work in the fields to keep our sanity and our beds warm and bring beauty into our lives. That was not being an artist. That was being alive."

10. When the sun went down and it was time for us to leave, the remembered little man just settling inside himself, and took on the look of the sunflowers in the field as if he were one of them. The women were finished piecing now. "We need to stop and smell the flowers sometimes," they said. "Now we can do our real quilting, our real art; making this world piece up right."

11. "I got to get back to the first yet, so important [...] fighting for freedom [...] Rosa working in civil [...] lynch. Mary Bethune c[...] making money fixing [...]

THE SUNFLOWERS QUILTERS SOCIETY OF AMERICA   ARLES FRANCE   AUGUST 22, 1991

AN INTERNATIONAL SYMBOL OF OUR DEDICATION TO CHANGE THE WORLD

The Sunflower Quilting Bee at Arles, 1991

The Quilting Bee at Arles

A thing I've always wanted to do was paint in the French Post-Impressionist manner and in this one I did. Willia Marie entertains a group of famous African-American women who are going all over the world having quilting bees. Here they are in Arles.

Sojourner Truth (c.1797-1883) spoke out against slavery and for women's rights.

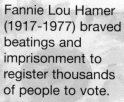

Fannie Lou Hamer (1917-1977) braved beatings and imprisonment to register thousands of people to vote.

Madame C. J. Walker (1867-1919) developed a hair-straightening preparation and became the first self-made American-born woman millionaire, employing over 3,000 people. She left more than half her fortune to charitable and educational causes.

Ida Wells (1862-1931) was a journalist who exposed the horrors of lynching in the South through writing and lecturing. She founded anti-lynching societies and women's clubs throughout the United States.

Harriet Tubman (c.1820-1913) brought over 300 slaves to freedom on the Underground Railroad during the time of slavery. During the Civil War she served as a spy for the Union Army.

Mary McLeod Bethune (1875-1955) was an educator who founded a college for black Americans and was a special adviser to President Franklin Roosevelt.

Rosa Parks (1913-) was arrested in 1955 for refusing to give up her seat on a segregated bus to a white man, which helped launch the civil rights movement.

Ella Baker (1905-1986) improved housing, jobs, and consumer education through her active involvement in many civil rights organizations.

Vincent van Gogh

(1853-1890) produced most of his work during a brief ten-year career. He is considered a genius for his originality—his use of brilliant colors, broken brush strokes, thick paint, and swirling lines that make his work look as if it is moving. His paintings are full of emotion.

Some of his most exciting work was done in Arles, a town in southern France. He often worked day and night, turning out one masterpiece after another: portraits, landscapes, and still lifes.

Van Gogh had a very sad life. During his lifetime he sold only one painting and was never recognized for his work. He suffered from mental illness and finally committed suicide.

Is there anything van Gogh has in common with Willia Marie or the women who are quilting?

What part of the painting looks as if it was done in van Gogh's style?

Find the part of the painting that looks like quilting.

Reproduce a quilt square with the sunflower pattern. Think about how different these sunflowers are from those done in van Gogh's style.

In *The Sunflower Quilting Bee at Arles*, the Dutch painter Vincent van Gogh has come to see the black women sewing in the sunflower fields. "Who is this strange-looking man?" they ask. "He is *un grand peintre* (a great painter)," Willia Marie tells them, "though he is greatly troubled in his mind."

Vincent van Gogh, *Self-portrait*, 1887

The women ask Willia Marie why she came to France—"Is this a natural setting for a black woman?"

Willia Marie replies that she came to France to seek opportunity, because it was not possible for her to be an artist in the United States.

The women answer, "We are all artists. Piecing is our art. We brought it straight from Africa. . . . We did it after a hard day's work in the fields to keep our sanity and our beds warm and bring beauty to our lives."

Vincent van Gogh, *Sunflowers*, 1888

I put the women together as quilters to say that they are piecing together freedom in this country. "Now we can do our real quilting, our real art—making this world piece up right."

What could the quilters "piece up" now? Can you think of some things that would bring freedom to the world? **If you were going to gather together people you admire, whom would you invite?** (They can be people from another time or place, or people living today.) Where would you go together? What would you be doing? Why would you choose these particular people?

Who's Afraid of **A**unt **J**emima ?

I want to use my art to express my feelings and ideas about the world.

You know, we create stereotypes—certain people are good, certain people are bad, certain people are lazy. . . . In *Who's Afraid of Aunt Jemima?* (my first story quilt), I retold the story of Aunt Jemima, who was supposed to be a stereotype of the black woman—as a cook, a servant, a maid taking care of her employer's children. In this work I turned Aunt Jemima into Jemima Blakey, a successful businesswoman.

So what does it take for people to realize that we don't all have to be alike and that for people to be different is wonderful and fine?

It does not affect your life at all that somebody else is a different religion, different color, different race, eats different kinds of food, dresses in different kinds of clothes, and so on. . . .

A stereotype: this image of the black woman as a cook and a housekeeper was used to sell pancake mix.

How are you different from other people? How are you like other people?

38

Of course, America has always been a multicultural society. First the Native Americans were here; then came everybody else. And since nobody's leaving, I guess that's the way it's going to have to be. I think that is one of the things that makes America wonderful.

It takes a certain amount of growth to allow yourself to be exposed to another person's culture. You have to have a kind of readiness to accept that another person's culture is as significant to them as yours is to you.

Crown Heights Children's History Story Quilt, 1994

That's what I was trying to get across in the Crown Heights quilt. Crown Heights is an area of Brooklyn where there has been fighting and even killings between two different groups of people. In the quilt there are twelve squares, one for each of the different cultures in Crown Heights. Each square illustrates a folktale or a story from that culture.

I use this excerpt from a poem by Langston Hughes:

I've known rivers:
I've known rivers ancient as the world
*   and older than the flow of human blood in human veins.*
My soul has grown deep like the rivers.

This poem is about the ancient African civilizations from which the African-American slave came, and about the power of knowing one's history. Each culture has its own stories that help you learn about them. And when you get all these people together, you benefit from their positive side. You benefit from the greatness of their cultures. Because that's what culture is—it's what your people did to survive.

Jamaicans (1950)
Anansi Stories

Haitians (1958)
The Banza

Are there special stories or poems that tell more about your history and who you are? Choose one and create a drawing about it. You might want to make the writing part of the picture the way Faith Ringgold does. **Research the different cultures in your own community.** Find out more about them. How many different groups of people live around you? Where are they from?

Puerto Ricans (1917)
The Rainbow-Colored Horse

ree West Africans (1626)
he Negro Speaks of Rivers

West African slaves (1626)
We Wear the Mask

Dutch (1624)
The Ghost of Peg Leg Peter

Algonquins (3000 B.C.)
The Winged Head

Mohawks (1920)
Bright Morning and Runs Fast

Italians (1835)
Catharine the Wise

ews (1654)
The Lost Princess

Vietnamese (1975)
Sea/Mountain Spirits

Koreans (1960)
Which Is Witch?

Personal Conviction

I can do anything. Nothing is going to stop me in my life and I'm going to pursue anything that turns me on. I'm *not* going to hear "No." If I want to achieve something, if it excites me—I can do it.

Do you think that this picture expresses Faith Ringgold's personal conviction? What do you see that makes you think so?

What a lot of people have to learn is to take negativity and turn it into something positive. It's a hard thing to learn, but that's what makes you not just a fighter but a winner!

You have to stick with it. You can't stop. That's the key. Do not stop. Continue. Persevere. Stay in there and you will get it.

Think about something that you really wanted to do, something that took a long time for you to accomplish. Or interview somebody who accomplished something in this way. Write or draw about this challenge. **What are your dreams?** What do you want to do or be? Will you succeed? How will you do it? **Write about and illustrate your plans.**

44

The Winner, 1988

Books by Faith Ringgold

Tar Beach (New York: Crown Publishers, 1991).
Aunt Harriet's Underground Railroad in the Sky (New York: Crown Publishers, 1992).
Dinner at Aunt Connie's House (New York: Hyperion, 1993).
My Dream of Martin Luther King (New York: Crown Publishers, 1995).
We Flew Over the Bridge: The Memoirs of Faith Ringgold (Boston: Little, Brown, 1995).

Videos about Faith Ringgold

Faith Ringgold: The Last Story Quilt and *Faith Ringgold Paints Crown Heights* produced by Linda
   Freeman. Color, 28 minutes each. L&S Video, Chappaqua, New York.
Tar Beach, with Faith Ringgold produced by Rosemary Keller. Color, 15 minutes. Scholastic, New York.

Works by Faith Ringgold
are housed in these museums and public collections:

Atlanta, Georgia: The Coca-Cola Company
Atlanta, Georgia: High Museum of Art
Boston, Massachusetts: Boston Museum of Fine Arts
Bronx, New York: Eugenio María de Hostos Community College
Brooklyn, New York: Brooklyn Children's Museum
Chicago, Illinois: Harold Washington Library center
Fort Wayne, Indiana: Fort Wayne Museum of Art
Lawrence, Kansas: Spencer Museum of Art
New York, New York: American Craft Museum
New York, New York: Chase Manhattan Bank Art Program
New York, New York: Metropolitan Museum of Art
New York, New York: Metropolitan Transit Authority
New York, New York: Museum of Modern Art
New York, New York: Philip Morris Collection
New York, New York: Solomon R. Guggenheim Museum
New York, New York: Studio Museum in Harlem
Newark, New Jersey: Newark Museum
Philadelphia, Pennsylvania: ARCO Chemical Company
Philadelphia, Pennsylvania: Philadelphia Museum of Art
St. Louis, Missouri: St. Louis Art Museum
Washington, D.C.: American Association of Retired Persons
Williamstown, Massachusetts: Williams College Museum of Art

Works in this book by Faith Ringgold

Café des Artistes. The French Collection, Part I, 1991. Acrylic paint on canvas, pieced fabric. 79 ½" x 90". Collection of the artist. (Page 27.)

Crown Heights Children's History Story Quilt. 1994. Acrylic paint on canvas, pieced fabric. 108" x 144". New York City Board of Education. (Page 41.)

Dancing at the Louvre. The French Collection, Part I, 1991. Acrylic paint on canvas, pieced fabric. 73" x 80". Collection of the artist. (Page 28.)

Dinner at Gertrude Stein's. The French Collection, Part I, 1991. Acrylic paint on canvas, pieced fabric. 79" x 84". Collection of the artist. (Page 27.)

Flag Is Bleeding, The. 1967. Oil paint on canvas. 72" x 96". Collection of the artist. (Page 22.)

Martin Luther King. 1975. Sewn fabric, acrylic paint, beads, wig hair, and embroidery. 72" high. Collection of the artist. (Page 14.)

Matisse's Chapel. The French Collection, Part I, 1991. Acrylic paint on canvas, pieced fabric. 74" x 79". Collection of the artist. (Page 27.)

Mrs. Jones and Family. The Family of Woman mask series, 1973. Sewn fabric, beads, and embroidery. 60" x 12" x 16". Collection of the artist. (Page 15.)

On the Beach at St. Tropez. The French Collection, Part I, 1991. Acrylic paint on canvas, pieced fabric. 74" x 92". Collection of the artist. (Page 27.)

Sonny's Quilt. 1986. Acrylic paint on canvas, pieced fabric. 84" x 60". Collection of Barbara and Ronald Balsar. (Page 18.)

Sunflower Quilting Bee at Arles, The. The French Collection, Part I, 1991. Acrylic paint on canvas, pieced fabric. 74" x 80". Private collection. (Page 32.)

Tar Beach. Woman on a Bridge series, 1988. Acrylic paint on canvas, pieced fabric. 74" x 69". Solomon R. Guggenheim Museum, New York City. (Page 5.)

Wedding on the Seine. The French Collection, Part I, 1991. Acrylic paint on canvas, pieced fabric. 74" x 89". Collection of the artist. (Page 27.)

Who's Afraid of Aunt Jemima? 1983. Acrylic paint on canvas, pieced fabric. 90" x 80". Collection of Fred Collins, Esq. (Page 40.)

Winner, The. Woman on a Bridge series, 1988. Acrylic paint on canvas, pieced fabric. 68" x 68". The Harold Washington Library. (Page 45.)

About the Authors

Linda Freeman was born in Greenwich Village in New York City in 1941. She studied at Tyler School of Fine Arts and at the Art Students League. A painter and a film producer, she is best known for her award-winning documentary film and video series on African-American artists. She is married to Sheldon Freeman and has two sons, Jon and Ross.

Faith Ringgold was born in Harlem in 1930. She graduated from the City College of New York's School of Education and was an art teacher before she began painting professionally during the 1960s. During the 1970s, she began incorporating beads and fabric into her work, and in 1980 she created her first painted quilt, *Echoes of Harlem,* in collaboration with her mother, Willi Posey. In *Who's Afraid of Aunt Jemima?* (1983) she incorporated a written story into one of her quilts for the first time. Since then, she has made more than 75 painted "story quilts." *Tar Beach*, Faith Ringgold's first book for children, based on a story quilt of the same name, won the Coretta Scott King Award for Illustration and was named a 1992 Caldecott Honor Book. She is married to Burdette Ringgold and has two daughters, Barbara and Michelle Wallace, and three granddaughters, Faith, Teddy, and Martha.

Nancy Roucher was born in St. Joseph, Missouri, in 1938. She received a bachelor's degree in journalism from the University of Missouri and a master's degree in aesthetic education from Sangamon State University. She developed a nationally recognized program in arts education that reached more than 125 schools in the Midwest and is currently co-director of the Florida Institute for Art Education, one of six regional sites with primary funding from the Getty Center for Education in the Arts, designed to assist teachers in implementing quality art education programs. Ms. Roucher lives in Sarasota. She is married to Jerry Roucher and has two daughters, Roslyn and Barbara.

Index

NAUSET REG.H.S. LIBRARY

30809000056091

709.2
RIN
Ringgold

Ringgold, Faith.
Talking to Faith
Ringgold

DATE DUE			

NAUSET REG. H.S. LIBRARY
P.O. BOX 1887   CABLE RD.
NORTH EASTHAM, MA 02651